Indian
an...
Leger...

Illustration by
Tapas Guha

Rupa • Co

First Published 2001
Second impression 2004

Published by
Rupa & Co
7/16, Ansari Road, Daryaganj,
New Delhi 110 002

Sales Centres:

Allahabad Bangalore Chandigarh Chennai
Hyderabad Jaipur Kathmandu
Kolkata Mumbai Pune

ISBN 81-7167-428-3

Typeset by
Nikita Overseas Pvt Ltd,
1410 Chiranjiv Tower,
43 Nehru Place
New Delhi 110 019

Printed in India by
Gopsons Papers Ltd.
A-14 Sector 60
Noida 201 301

Contents

Contents

Debjani Chatterjee

Hanuman and the Sun God

HANUMAN, the monkey-god, is a very popular Indian hero who figures in countless stories in slightly different guises all over Asia. This is the story of his miraculous birth and of his childhood.

On earth, the king and queen of the monkeys were troubled. Anjana, the most beautiful monkey in their forest kingdom, was always sad and would never smile. Most unnatural of all, she avoided the company of other monkeys. "She is too proud to mix with us," they said, and some of them pulled faces at her.

Anjana was once a happy goddess in Indraloka — the glorious heaven where Indra reigns. But as ill luck would have it, she angered a holy man whose curse turned her into a monkey who would have to live on Earth. Now it seemed she could not forget her previous existence and missed the company of the gods and goddesses who had been her friends. Oh, how she hated being a monkey!

"Anjana," said the monkey queen, "we wish you could be happy. We monkeys are naturally gay and carefree. Be one of us and you shall have an honoured place in our kingdom. Forget Indraloka. We will gladly arrange your marriage with one of our monkeys, if you want, and then you will no longer be lonely."

"Yes, sister," added the king, "enough of this moping! The holy man who cursed you must have been a fool — he wanted to turn you into something ugly and to be laughed at, but he did not succeed. For we monkeys are handsome and noble animals. Come now, it is surely a matter of pride to be a monkey! And you are lucky to be such a beautiful and gifted one. You have so much to teach us. My queen's suggestion of marriage is an excellent idea. You should have children, Anjana. They would add to the strength of our kingdom. Now leave us and come back only when you have thought seriously about this matter."

Anjana thanked the royal monkeys. "I know you mean well, and I am grateful. But I have no wish to marry — it is not that I think monkeys are ugly (she did really, but had no wish to hurt their feelings), I just need more time to adjust to this life. But do not ask me to forget Indraloka, it is my true home and someday I hope to return to it."

Poor Anjana wandered through the forest. When she was tired she lay down on the grassy top of a hill. Here the cool breeze soothed her and she soon fell asleep.

Vayu, the god of the wind, was about his daily business of blowing through the world, when he saw a beautiful monkey and found himself drawn towards her. He realised at once that this was no ordinary monkey. Using his magic powers he quickly unraveled the truth about Anjana.

"Anjana," he whispered, lightly caressing her monkey body. Anjana sighed in her dream-like state and, becoming bolder, the wind-god gently caught her sigh in a kiss.

Startled, Anjana sat up quickly. "Who did that? Who calls my name? Show yourself." She looked around, but could see no one.

"Don't be afraid," said a deep voice all around her. "I am Vayu, the wind. Seeing your beauty I could not help kissing you. It is my wish to give you a son."

"Vayu, your nature is always playful and boisterous. Have pity and stop this teasing. Can't you see that I am a monkey now? No one can be beautiful in this form. I certainly want no children who will look like me. Go away."

"Anjana, if you see yourself with my eyes you would realise just how lovely you are. My wish is very strong and it is already done. I have given you a mighty son. Born of my breath, he is the child of our two spirits joined together in your dream. Look, there he lies at your feet!"

The children of gods are born instantly. Anjana saw that smiling at her was the cutest baby monkey. It stretched out its little arms and made gurgling noises. Something inside Anjana melted. She picked up the baby in delight. "It is true after all," she exclaimed, "monkeys are handsome and noble creatures!"

Vayu laughed when he heard this.

"I must leave you now, dear Anjana, and go about my duties. But I give you my son, Hanuman. Look after him well."

Anjana had eyes only for her wonderful baby. Three times did Vayu circle around the mother and the child and blessed them with these words: "I gift you my strength, my son. Be the strongest in the world. I gift you my speed, my son. Be the fastest in the world. I gift you my power to fly, my son. Be a mighty hero who will bring much happiness to your mother."

With the baby Hanuman in her arms, Anjana presented herself once more to the monkey king and queen. They greeted her with joy and all the monkeys congratulated Anjana on her splendid baby. Even though her son was no ordinary monkey — having the Wind for his father and a goddess-monkey for his mother — the kind monkeys accepted her as one of themselves and made much of the baby. Older monkeys gave her plenty of advice on bringing him up.

Hanuman was full of mischief as a child and Anjana found it extremely difficult to control him. "You are just like the wind," she would say in despair at times, "how can one hold you?"

The fact that he had extraordinary powers made things both easy and difficult for his mother. Once while standing on a mountain-top Anjana had a sudden fright and dropped Hanuman by accident. To her horror the baby fell a great distance down the mountain-side and landed on his head. But then he just bounced straight back into her arms, none the worse for his fall! The rock on which he fell, however, was shattered into a thousand pieces — such was his power!

While still very little, Hanuman discovered that he could fly. Now there was simply no holding him back! His curiosity and sense of adventure led him to explore many far away and dangerous places. He made friends with all the

forest animals and, knowing him to be only a child (and a strong one!), they were very patient with him and put up with a lot of his mischief. He would race the eagle in the sky. At monkey assemblies he would play tricks on some of the solemn elders and tie their tails together!

One day Hanuman looked up at the sun which appeared to him like a glowing red ball in the sky.

"Oh! I must have that ball to play with," thought the little monkey and straightaway leapt into the sky.

Terrified at the strange sight of a flying monkey who was coming to grab him Surya, the sun-god, fled. But Hanuman was determined to chase him. The faster the sun fled, the faster flew the monkey and he did not seem to tire at all. The world spun round and round till everyone felt dizzy and confused.

"Protect me, Indra," cried the sun at last, panting with exhaustion.

The king of the gods, disturbed from his pleasures, was not at all amused to see what was going on.

"That wretched monkey must be taught a lesson!" decided Indra. In his anger, he let loose his thunderbolt to bring down the flying creature. Hit hard in the chest by Indra's dreaded weapon, Hanuman fell unconscious from the sky.

It was in this pitiful state that Vayu found him. The god of the wind set up a terrible howling gale all over the earth. Then when his anger had cooled a little, Vayu picked up the monkey-child in his arms and took him inside a mountain cave. Here he sat and brooded. No longer did he blow about the world. Soon all creatures began to struggle for breath because each day there was less and less air for them to breathe. Plants began to wilt and die.

"Unless Vayu does his work, there will soon be no life left on earth," said the gods, greatly concerned.

They knew that Vayu was annoyed with Indra, their king, so they went to one who was greater than Indra — Brahma, the Creator of all life.

"Yes, my children, I will go to Vayu," assured Brahma, "but Indra must also come along and say that he is sorry, or Vayu will not give up his sulking."

The two gods appeared in front of Vayu who stood up and greeted them with respect.

"O mighty Wind, forgive Indra's mistake," said Brahma. "He punished your son in a moment's anger, not considering that the little one did not know that he was doing wrong. Indra has learnt that one must think before one acts, especially if one is a king — for when a king does wrong, where can his subjects find justice? But why should you now make a second mistake by punishing all living things on earth when they have done you no wrong?"

Indra, who is a proud god, hung his head in shame. Brahma loves little children and, taking Hanuman on his lap, he patted him. Instantly the monkey opened his eyes and sat up.

"Rise, my son," said Vayu, "and thank Brahma who is the father of us all and who has given you back your health. Now ask these noble gods for their blessings."

Like a well brought up child, Hanuman paid his respects, not only to Brahma, but also to Indra and to his father. Vayu was pleased to hear the two gods praise his son. "What courage he has, what speed and what strength!" cried Indra. "I am ashamed to have used my thunderbolt against a mere child. You have my blessing, Hanuman, that from this day onwards no weapon can injure you."

Brahma then gave the monkey-boy the gift of immortality, "Death shall not touch you. You will live forever, like the gods."

Indra, who was anxious to make up for having earlier wounded Hanuman with his thunderbolt, now gave him a very special power. Whenever he wanted, Hanuman could change his size — he could grow enormously big or shrink to the tiniest speck of dust!

"I am happy that you have blessed my son with so many gifts, but all these powers are useless and even dangerous to one who has no wisdom. I do not want Hanuman to engage anymore in such a foolishness as trying to catch the sun. I am afraid he is a great trial to his poor mother. Please bless him then with wisdom so that he may do only good deeds from now on."

"It shall be so," agreed Brahma graciously. "He will be the wisest of all monkeys. The monkey king will profit by his wise counsel. Now forgive your own king, Indra, and return to your duties."

"Vayu has already won so many gifts for his son," said Indra, "that we should perhaps leave before I end up giving away my throne!"

When the two visitors had left, Vayu told Hanuman to return to his mother and to use his powers well. Then the wind-god, mightily pleased, flew out of the cave and began to blow through the world again.

From now on the monkey-child began to show much wisdom in everything he did. He was still full of fun, but was also always thoughtful of others. He was generally quiet and very modest, always helping the weak and showing great respect to Anjana and other elder monkeys. He thought carefully before he spoke and his words were always gracious. Little wonder that he soon became much loved by all. The monkey king and queen made sure that Hanuman had the best education possible and he quickly learnt all that there was to know. When he grew to adulthood, Hanuman became the royal champion — his strength and courage being unequalled.

Recognising his rare intelligence and mastery of languages, the king appointed him his minister and sent him as his ambassador to neighbouring lands whenever any tricky negotiations were to be made. But in spite of his high position, Hanuman remained so humble and good-natured that none of the monkeys felt envious of him in any way.

Hanuman and his mother were very close. "Lucky Anjana! Our Hanuman is the best son any mother could hope to have," they said. Anjana felt that her heart would burst with joy and pride in her monkey-son.

DEBJANI CHATTERJEE

The Ninth Jewel

RAJA VIKRAMADITYA, a great king of India a long, long time ago, had 'nine jewels' at his court. These were the nine wisest people in the kingdom. They were called the nine jewels because Raja Vikramaditya believed that they were the real wealth of his nation. Each of these people has a place in history, but most famous of all is the ninth jewel, the writer Kalidas.

Not many know that Kalidas was in fact a simpleton for many years of his life. Kalidas had very little education to speak of. He could not do the simplest job properly and was such a fool that he would always get into trouble. Bullies would sometimes tease him.

The name Kalidas means servant of Kali, the black goddess. True to his name, Kalidas loved the goddess Kali and devoted his whole life serving her. People would not trust him with any serious task, but whatever he did, Kalidas did in Kali's name. Whether he was eating, drinking or even bathing he would first remember the name of Kali. In this way everything that he did became a prayer.

Kali is the goddess of endless time and contains all power. The dreaded destroyer of evil, she battles with ignorance, confusion and everything that makes slaves of people. But Kali is also a merciful mother to all who call her and this is how Kalidas thought of her. "You have the name of the goddess in your own," someone had told him in his childhood, "so ask her to bless you. Kali will never abandon one who is her servant." Kalidas believed this totally.

Being a simpleton, Kalidas was also desperately poor. He would do odd jobs for people, but these were of the simplest kind and often he could find no work. Although he was a strong and handsome young man, he could not find himself a wife either. But Kalidas was never sorry for himself. He trusted that the goddess would find him the right partner. He would smile a lot and sing of Mother Kali. Since his memory was poor, he could not remember the complete song but he would sing a few lines that came into his head.

One fine day Kalidas armed himself with an axe and climbed a tall tree. He crawled along one of the branches and sat facing the tree trunk, swinging his legs down either side of the branch. Lifting his axe Kalidas began to strike at the branch. "Mother Kali, bless your servant!" sang Kalidas as he worked.

In a very short while he was interrupted from below. "O Kalidas, what are you doing?" called a passer-by.

"I am chopping this branch," explained Kalidas, mopping his forehead. "It is a nice large branch, so when I have chopped it all up I shall be able to sell it for firewood."

By this time quite a big crowd had gathered. "Don't you realise, you fool," said someone, "that you are about to kill yourself? Everyone knows that you should sit facing away from the tree when you are cutting its branch. Now the branch is already cracking and if you strike it once more it will fall to the ground and you will fall with it!"

Kalidas kept looking from the crowd to the crack in the branch and again to his axe. Then he agreed that they were right. "Yes, I am an idiot," he admitted. "Everyone says so. How I wish I was not a fool!"

But the people below him were now deep in conversation among themselves. "This is the very man, my friend!" said one of them in an excited voice. "Through him we can be revenged on Kamala."

It so happened that the men were all learned people who had been walking away from a public debate with Kamala — a woman of great learning. One by one they had each tried to compete with her in argument, but they had all failed. They were poor losers and were upset at losing to a woman. "It is not fair that she is not only learned, but is also young and beautiful!" said one man. "They say she is awfully proud of her learning," said another. "King Vikramaditya is always praising her." "She has vowed that she will only marry the man who can defeat her in argument," said a third. Each of the learned men had tried to win the debate in the hope of marrying Kamala.

The men now plotted to trick Kamala into admitting defeat to the biggest fool in the kingdom. "It will serve her right if she gets married to an idiot!" they said. "Let us tell Kalidas that we have come to arrange his marriage to Kamala."

Kalidas was overjoyed. These kind men were offering to arrange his marriage to the most beautiful and most learned woman in the land! Truly, he must have the blessing of Mother Kali, he thought. He agreed to do exactly as the men told him.

When Kamala was told that a man of great learning had just arrived in the kingdom, she became eager to meet him. It did not take much persuasion on the part of Kalidas's new friends to make Kamala invite him to a debate.

The day of the contest arrived. Kalidas was dressed with great care to look his best. He was very happy — he had been told that it would be his wedding day. The entire crowd of learned men accompanied him to Kamala's house.

"Kamala, on this day of the week the learned Kalidas is in the habit of keeping a vow of silence," explained one of the men. "But he has come anyway, so as not to disappoint you."

"Oh, there can be no debate then!" said Kamala, looking sadly at Kalidas. But Kalidas shook his head. He had been told to do this and to keep his mouth shut the whole day.

"The learned Kalidas is telling you that even without speaking he can debate with you!" said the others. So the strange contest between the fool and the woman of learning began. Kamala sat at one side of the room and Kalidas at another. The other learned men who were all helping Kalidas sat behind Kamala so that they could make signs with their hands for Kalidas to imitate without Kamala knowing.

Kamala recited a beautiful but difficult poem in Sanskrit which was a language that all learned

people knew in those days. Of course Kalidas did not know any Sanskrit, but he smiled and nodded. Kamala lifted one finger and said to Kalidas that she believed that God was one. The fool immediately raised two fingers in imitation of the learned men who then began to loudly praise him. "What does he mean?" asked Kamala in surprise. "Why, Kamala, he is saying that to the believer God and he are two," explained someone.

In this way Kamala asked many questions, but Kalidas always answered them, sometimes with the motion of his hands and sometimes with that of his head. The room full of learned men kept convincing Kamala that every one of his answers was brilliant. This went on for quite a while, until Kamala accepted that she had finally met her match, and agreed to marry Kalidas that very day.

Kalidas had fallen in love with Kamala the moment he saw her. But as soon as it was nighttime and the period of his silence was over, Kamala discovered to her horror that she had been tricked into marrying someone who was in fact a fool. Her pride was hurt and she was extremely angry.

Although Kalidas himself had not intended to trick her, she refused to have anything to do with him, and pushed him out of the house. When Kalidas told her that he loved her and that he was her husband, Kamala said scornfully that a fool who did not even know Sanskrit could never be her husband. "Unless you can change into a man of great learning who can write books in Sanskrit, don't bother coming back to me!" she said.

Poor Kalidas! He was no longer a happy and carefree person. His face was always worried and sad now. Determined to make himself a fit husband for Kamala, he went from one teacher to another and begged them to teach him Sanskrit. He wanted to read the many holy books of the Hindus. But he simply could not understand what he was taught. He tried very hard but it was useless. "Even an ass would be a better pupil than you!" said his teachers, giving up on him.

At last Kalidas came to believe that he could never become a learned man and that his wife was lost to him forever. In complete misery he decided to end his life by drowning in the river. He began to walk into the water. Just then he heard a voice calling him. Kalidas turned around and saw a little girl on the river bank. "Kalidas, you have been reading the holy books," she said to him, "don't they tell you that it is wrong to commit suicide?"

"How should I know?" replied Kalidas bitterly. "I am a fool and cannot understand any books. This is how Mother Kali has made me. But there is no room in the world for an idiot like me, so I am putting an end to my misery. I have called on the goddess often enough to bless me and she gave me a wonderful wife who is like Saraswati, the goddess of learning. But this blessing was wasted on me. If only I was a man of learning!"

"Then it shall be so," said the little girl. "Kalidas, my son, I shall remove the darkness of ignorance from you forever!"

Even as Kalidas rubbed his eyes, the little girl was transformed. Saraswati, the goddess of learning, stood on the river bank. Kalidas rushed out of the river and knelt at her feet, his mouth open in wonder. The goddess gently touched his tongue. "The most beautiful poetry in Sanskrit will come from your mouth, Kalidas, and from your pen," blessed Saraswati. For Kalidas it was as though he saw the whole world properly for the first time. Wisdom flooded in.

"Kalidas the fool walked into the river," said the goddess, "but you have come out now as Kalidas, the wisest and most learned man in the land!"

In great joy Kalidas returned to his wife who marvelled to find him changed so suddenly. He was now an ocean of wisdom and knowledge. She was ashamed of her earlier bad temper and rude treatment of him. With her loving and constant support Kalidas became a busy writer and wrote many books of poetry and drama. He is remembered today as the greatest playwright in the Sanskrit language and one of the world's best poets.

Kalidas's fame spread throughout the land. When King Vikramaditya who loved learning called Kamala one day to his palace to recite some of her work, she insisted on reciting some of her husband's poetry instead. This greatly impressed the king who wished to meet the author. It was not long before a royal chariot appeared at Kalidas's door. Raja Vikramaditya had come to personally invite the poet to come and live at his court. "I have eight jewels at my court, Kalidas," said the king, "some of the finest minds in the kingdom. They are my advisers so that I can govern with wisdom for the benefit of my people. I need you to come and join them. I will give you everything you could possibly want to carry on with your writing. Be the ninth and most splendid jewel at my court."

Kalidas and Kamala went to live in the palace. Vikramaditya's rule was a golden age. His people were at peace and they prospered in every way. It was their claim that while they had great wealth and power, they also had nine special jewels in their kingdom and the brightest of these was Kalidas.

SUDHIN N. GHOSE

The Story of Nischoy Datta
of Ujjain

NISCHOY DATTA of Ujjain was an actor by profession. He was a handsome fellow and certainly a clever player, though he was addicted to the strange practice of putting a mudpack on his face every morning before bathing in the Sipra River.

People made fun of his foible. Some laughed, while others jeered. A few declared that he was exceptionally vain. His friends and admirers explained, "He is a bit crazy about wrinkles on his face. Otherwise there is nothing particularly wrong with him."

So to avoid all unpleasantness Nischoy finally chose a less-frequented bend of the river, far from the city; and there he lay for hours at a stretch, wallowing in the mud like a blind turtle with his back exposed to the morning sun and his face thrust into the oozy slime of the Sipra. No one came there to crack jokes at his expense, for the place was said to be haunted. Near it stood the forbidding temple of Maha Kala — the dark deity of time — whose worshippers were none other than the wizards and witches and others of their sort, whom all decent citizens shunned like the plague.

"Nischoy," said his friends one day, "are you not afraid of the Maha Kala temple?"

"Whatever for?" he asked innocently.

"Well," they explained, "you may not believe in black magic; but, to tell you the truth, the shrine is the haunt of Mountain Yakshas at night. And one early morning you may come across some of these night prowlers, and they will surely change you into a ram."

"Let them try," Nischoy replied, shrugging his shoulders.

The next day long before dawn, when it was still dark, Nischoy went to his favourite bathing site, and had a good laugh when he felt a pair of hands rubbing oil on his bare back as he lay on his stomach with his face covered with his mudpack.

"Who is it?" he asked without turning round. "Is it a Yaksha by any chance?"

"No, not a Yaksha," came the reply, "but daughter of a Yaksha. I am called Nanda."

"The Yaksha must be lucky," said Nischoy, "to have a daughter like Nanda, one with such a sweet voice and such soft hands."

"Flatterer," Nanda murmured.

"Flattery or no flattery," Nischoy went on, "it is really kind of you to massage my back. As a rule," he added, "I smear a pillar of the Maha Kala temple with oil and then rub my back against it."

"And that's how you have made the rough stone smooth like polished alabaster."

"The feel of your hands is like alabaster, and you have such a lovely voice. You ought to be a great success on the stage."

"Who would care to see a daughter of a Yaksha act?"

"Tell me another," Nischoy said and roared with laughter. He simply refused to believe that a daughter of a Mountain Yaksha was massaging his back. So he finally added, "I presume you can fly through the air like all Yakshas! And change me into a ram if you want to!"

"Of course I can."

"Then wait a minute. Let me remove my mudpack and see what this daughter of a Mountain Yaksha looks like."

But by the time he had removed the covering from his face and turned round, the unknown lady was gone: she was not by his side. Nischoy looked for her in the temple, but it was empty as usual. He searched for her among the groves on the river bank, but she was not there. He looked in vain for her among the clumps of reeds. He sought for her everywhere, but there was not the slightest trace of her anywhere — not even her footprints: Nanda had simply vanished.

Who could she be? Perhaps, Nischoy thought, some actress was here to play a trick on me. Then he mused, "I know every one of them, and all of them are vixens. Tell them something nice and they will snarl back. It is best to forget all about this so-called daughter of a Yaksha."

But try as he would the melody of the sweet voice of this unseen woman kept ringing in his ears. He went about as though in a dream, paying little attention to what was happening round him, and thinking all the while of her.

"Nischoy has changed," his friends whispered. "Is he sick?"

"The roaring bull has become a mooning calf," remarked his rivals, those who were jealous of his good looks and accomplished acting: "Nischoy is lovesick."

And that was the case. He was in love with Nanda, the unknown person who had rubbed his back, though he did not know what she looked like. He went back to his favourite place — not once, but many, many times — but no one ever came to talk to him as he lay turtlewise in the mud; no hand massaged his back.

Then one day something unexpected happened. As he was rubbing his back against one of the columns of the Maha Kala temple he felt, though no one was there, the timid touch of a pair of furtive hands. It seemed as though an invisible being was trying to help him on with his massage. It was a queer feeling, and Nischoy closed his eyes to make sure that he was not imagining things. "No," he said to himself, after some reflection, "there is no mistake. Someone is by my side. Maybe, a ghost. All the same, I am going to catch hold of the ghost's hands." No sooner thought than done. When Nischoy opened his eyes he gasped in amazement: there was no one to be seen, nevertheless he felt in his grasp an invisible girl who was struggling hard to set herself free.

"Let go of my hand!" cried the invisible girl. "You are hurting me. I have done you no harm. Please let go of my hand." Nischoy recognised at once that it was the voice of Nanda, the daughter of the Yakshas — the cause of his lovesickness.

"No," he said, "I won't let you go. You have made me suffer cruelly. Make yourself visible, Nanda."

"I can't," said Nanda. "Really, I can't."

"Why not? If you belong to the Yakshas you can make yourself visible or invisible at will."

That was true, the Yaksha girl admitted. "But," she pleaded, "I am wearing nothing just now. My clothes are on the river bank. How can I appear naked before you?"

Nischoy declared that he did not care whether she was stark naked or fully clothed. He was in love with her and that was the thing that mattered most to him. And Nanda shyly murmured that the same was the case with her. "Then," he asked, "why have you made me suffer? Why did you come just once and then vanish for good?"

"Vanish for good!" Nanda protested, "O, no. I have usually been by your side all these days, though you did not see me. I have also suffered a lot on your account. My father is simply furious, for he knows I am in love with you. 'A handsome man,' he says, 'is a faithless man. And then whoever has heard of a pretty Yaksha princess marrying a human actor however good-looking he may be? There you have my story." She then added with a sigh, "Today is my last day of freedom. I have to return to my father's palace in

Pushkar before dark and stay there a prisoner till I get married or die a spinster."

To this Nischoy said, "What prevents you from marrying me? And making yourself as well as me happy?"

"Nothing, except that you should ask my father for my hand. This is the promise I have given him." After a pause she murmured, "Do you think you love me enough to take the long journey to Pushkar, the city of the Mountain Yakshas? It is on a ridge of the Himalayas."

Nischoy vowed that he was ready to go to the end of the earth for Nanda's sake. All that she had to do was to indicate the way to Pushkar and wait there for his arrival. Upon which, she made herself visible, and he saw that she was beautiful in every limb, far more graceful than the most elegant actress of Ujjain; and his love for her increased.

They spent the whole day together, talking to each other, discussing their future plans. Hours flew past without their knowing. At sunset they came to their senses, so to speak, for it was high time for Nanda to return to Pushkar: her last day of freedom was at an end. They hurriedly exchanged their rings, and Nanda flew up in the air and departed for her home, while Nischoy slowly walked back to Ujjain, sad at heart and yet grateful and glad for having known Nanda.

The next morning Nischoy did not go to his usual bathing place, but joined a group of three Deccani merchants who were travelling north. The journey was uneventful till they reached the hilly northern regions, and there a swift stroke of misfortune made Nischoy and his three companions prisoners of the Tajikis. The Tajikis were a wild race of hunters, who occasionally raided the peaceful caravanserais of neighbouring lands at night to capture able-bodied men and sell them as slaves in Tajikistan and Turkistan.

"Now we are finished," moaned the three Deccani merchants. "We shall have to end our days as slaves of these savages."

"Nothing of the sort," replied Nischoy. "You asked me the other day, 'What is an actor good for?' Now you will have the answer. I have picked up their password. It took me less than a minute to master it and a few other things besides. Just explain to me the way to Pushkar, and I shall see to it that we are set free when they change guards."

The way to Pushkar, they said, was easy to find: one had to cross the Vitasta river and th strike due north.

"Many thanks," said Nischoy. And when the Tajiki guards were changed he went boldly to the new sentinels and whispered to them the password he had picked up and pointed to the three Deccani merchants.

"Are you one of our spies?" they asked.

"Yes," replied Nischoy. "Those three are my stooges. We want to explore the lie of the land for tonight's raid."

"Then go by all means," they said and complemented Nischoy on his excellent command of the Tajiki language.

"By the way," they added, "the password may be changed by midday. Just in case you happen to be late you had better learn by heart the formula *Non-Gon-Cho-Ko* .... It will see you through for all practical purposes."

That was how Nischoy Datta managed to come out of the Tajiki slave camp with his three companions. Once out of the danger zone the three merchants cursed loudly the Tajikis and all wild tribes engaged in the slave trade. They then told Nischoy, "My dear man, you are a splendid fellow. But you have a few screws loose in your head. Fancy thinking of climbing the Himalayas after an adventure like this. Are you mad? Don't you know that you will have to pass through the forests of Kashmir to reach Pushkar?"

"What's wrong with the forests of Kashmir?"

"They are full of wild animals," said one of the merchants. "And," added another, "what is worse, they are haunted by witches." "These witches," the third one explained, "are no ordinary witches. They are cannibals, real man-eaters, far worse than the Tajikis. You have saved us, and it is our duty to save you now. Give up the idea of going to Pushkar, and come along with us to Deccan. There you will find plenty of decent theatres and, we guarantee, your talents will not be wasted."

Nischoy, however, refused to be dissuaded from his journey. So the merchants gave up arguing with him and sighed, "Actors are difficult people. However," they added, "if go you must then take this piece of magic chalk with you. At night draw a circle with it around your bed. Then no witch will be able to get at you. And to keep the wild beasts out, don't forget to make a big fire." With this the merchants left for Deccan, and he travelled northwards.

As he went along he fell in with four conjurors. These men had shown one another all their tricks and were, by the time Nischoy overtook them, pretty well bored at not having any one to admire their sleight-of-hand. They were therefore delighted with his company and gave him a display of their entire repertory of legerdemain. "Now," they finally said, "let us have some magic tricks from you." Nischoy declared that he knew nothing about conjuring; but he had with him a piece of enchanted chalk which could be of service in keeping away witches from one's beside.

At this the conjurors laughed themselves hoarse. "Don't believe in old wives' tales," they counselled Nischoy. "We are grey-haired conjurors, and take it from us, there is no such thing as witchcraft. It is all done by sleight-of-hand. Only ignorant people believe in black art, in

witches, wizards, warlocks, and what not. A smart young fellow like yourself carrying a piece of magic chalk! You will make us die of laughter."

Their hilarity was, however, interrupted by some woodcutters. "Where are you going," the woodmen asked, "now the day is nearly over? There is no village before you, but only an empty temple of Siva. We would not advise you to spend the night there."

"Why not?" asked the conjurors.

"Whoever remains there during the night falls a prey to a witch. She makes horns grow on his forehead and then changes him into a stag." They believed that the witch was fond of venison. Once the forest was full of deer, but now there was not a single one to be seen. As there were no natural deer for the witch to devour she uses her magic power to change men into stags for her food. "It sounds strange," the woodmen ended, "but this is the case. We are local people, and we know all about this witch. She is called Dakini."

"Thank you," said the conjurors. "We are magicians ourselves and we want to have a word with Dakini. All the same, many thanks for your warning." They then whispered to Nischoy, who was hesitating, "Come along, young man. Don't listen to this nonsense. There are four of us to protect you. And then you have your wonderful magic chalk! What are you afraid of? We will make a big fire to keep the wild animals out. No witch is going to harm you so long as we are about."

As Nischoy still wavered they thumped him on the back and declared that they had spent many a night in haunted houses, abandoned temples, ancient cemeteries, and dismal cremation grounds, but nowhere had they found the least trace of any ghosts or witches. So he was finally induced to accompany them.

The empty temple of Siva was soon reached. They made a big fire in its flagstone courtyard. And when Nischoy drew a circle with his magic chalk to keep all witches out, the conjurors had another hearty laugh. "Young man," they guffawed, "you are not better than the ignorant woodmen. However, to please you we shall sleep in the middle of the circle with you."

Towards the end of the first watch of the night Nischoy, who was a light sleeper, was awakened by a faint sound of music coming from afar. He listened carefully. The music grew gradually louder and louder as it approached the temple. Then, still pretending to be fast asleep, he saw through the corner of one eye a weird woman, her body smeared with ashes and her hair unkempt, dancing about the courtyard as she played on a lute made of bone. Soon she quickened her steps and moved round and round the circular spot marked by Nischoy's magic chalk. She then began a strange song and fixed her gaze on one of the conjurors, who sat up and stared at her like some-one hypnotised.

"Dakini," this conjuror said after watching her for awhile, "I had a good mind at first to laugh at your antics, for I am in the same busi-ness as you. But now I feel like applauding. You are clever with your feet while I am skilled only in sleight-of-hand."

"Then," said the witch "come out of the chalk circle and join me. I shall teach you my steps and you will teach me your tricks with your hands."

Now as soon as the conjuror moved out of the magic enclosure horns began to sprout on his head for the witch was singing a horn-sprouting spell as she danced and played on her bone lute. Her magic formula had no effect on her victim as long as he was inside the chalk circle. The conjuror, however, was soon changed into a stag.

"Fine," Dakini exclaimed as she patted the stag. "Now go and join your fellows in my pen." The animal docilely obeyed her order and pranced out of the temple yard. She then started to play on her lute again and in the same manner as before transformed the other conjurors, one by one, into stags.

Now while she was patting her fourth victim, Nischoy stealthily got up and seized her lute which she had laid aside on the ground. He then crept back to the middle of the chalk circle. As he had hitherto pretended to be fast asleep it took the witch some time to realise her loss. By then, however, Nischoy was safely within the enchanted ring of chalk, and he now began to strum on the lute and repeat the horn-producing spell he had heard Dakini sing. Being a clever actor, he was, as has been said before, quick at picking up strange sayings and formulas and memorising them. His pronunciation too was faultless. The effect of the magic spell he intoned was immediate. Horns began to sprout out of Dakini's forehead.

At this she raised a piercing shriek. And then falling on her knees she cried, "Stop! My son, stop! Don't you know that the spell will change me into a hind? And that would be the end of me for then I shall have to give satisfaction to an entire herd of stags."

"What about it?" Nischoy said. "You are wicked enough to merit the worst punishment."

"If you knew my story, son," Dakini sobbed, "you would pity me instead of getting angry." She then recounted her tale, which in brief was this: constrained to serve as an instrument of destiny, she punished only those who merited punishment; were she destroyed before she had finished her assignment she would be reborn to end her unfinished task. "Believe me or not," she ended, "I am ready to do anything to please you. Only don't change me into a deer."

"Can you help me to reach Pushkar?"

"Of course, I can. Climb on my back, son, and I shall fly through the air like a winged horse. We shall soon be there."

And that was how Nischoy came to the royal city of the Mountain Yakshas, flying through the air, with Dakini as his mount. There he bade her goodbye.

Now the king of the Yakshas had passed a decree enjoining that the first man to enter his dominion that day was to be thrown down a high cliff and executed in this way, for some careless boys had sent a boulder rolling down a slope, and it had fallen in the midst of a picnic party of Yakshas and killed a number of them.

"Though the Yakshas can fly through the air," the Yaksha guards explained to Nischoy, "though they can become invisible at will, they suffer pain and death in the same way as men. In ancient times men were reasonable. Before dropping a bucket into a well," they went on, "men used to call out, 'Peace! Peace be with you!' This was a warning to the Yakshas in case they happened to be loitering at the bottom of the well. Then in later times men used to shout, 'Look out!' It was not a polite warning, nevertheless it was a warning. But nowadays what do they do? They just hurl a bucket into the well without any warning. No wonder your boys have become as bad as gnomes and goblins and," they ended, "you can't blame us for punishing you. It was a gang of your boys — human children — who maimed and killed a number of innocent Yakshas. And you as a human being must recognise your share of guilt."

Nischoy was dumbfounded at the unexpected turn of events at his journey's end. After long months of travail and trial he was within sight of the palace where Nanda lived, and now he was on the point of being executed without getting even a glimpse of her. He was in no mood to argue with the Yaksha guards who had taken him captive. He asked them, however, "Please can you tell me how Princess Nanda is doing?"

"She is at death's door," they sighed, "wasting in every limb on account of her love for a faithless human being, a member of your tribe. Our physicians have given up all hope." They then asked him, "Are you by any chance a doctor? If you can save Princess Nanda our king will surely grant you your life and reward you handsomely."

"I can try," said Nischoy as he took off from his finger the ring Nanda had given him. He then asked the guards to pass it on to her. "Its sight," he added, "will surely cure her." The ring, however, produced a contrary effect on the guards. Instead of being mollified, they declared angrily, "You are a thief. You must have stolen it from the king's treasury. It bears the royal coat of arms. How did you get it?" They simply refused to believe that it was Nanda herself who had exchanged the ring with Nischoy's.

"I swear," Nischoy cried, "Nanda herself gave it to me in the Maha Kala temple."

"How can we believe you when a moment ago you claimed to be a doctor? And now you are trying to explain that you are an actor."

"I am not a doctor," Nischoy said. "But I am capable of curing her all the same. Believe it or not, I know a few tricks that will make your flesh creep. Just give me my bone lute and let me sing a song, and you will see for yourself what I mean."

They began to laugh when Nischoy started to strum on the bone lute and sing his horn-producing spell. However, soon their mirth changed into consternation, for they found horns sprouting out of their foreheads. Fortunately, Nischoy did not proceed far with his incantation — just enough to give the guards tiny horns.

The news of this astonishing affair soon spread like wildfire in Pushkar. People accused the guards of misinterpreting the king's decree and foolishly detaining a human miracle-maker who had come all the way from Ujjain to cure their much loved Princess Nanda. The prime minister called on Nischoy to present him his apologies and read out to him the royal rescript promising Nanda's hand to whoever would cure her.

What happened next is easy to guess.

Nanda was restored the moment she saw Nischoy. Then came their marriage celebrations. Pushkar was brilliantly illuminated. The marriage contract imposed two conditions on Nischoy: one was stipulated by the Yaksha king, namely, Nanda should be allowed to spend the summer months every year in Pushkar; and the other — the bride's stipulation — insisted that Nischoy should take his bride as his partner on the stage. Of course, Nischoy readily accepted these two conditions.

The newly-wedded couple returned by air to Ujjain. Nanda, being a daughter of the Yakshas, knew, as we have already noticed, the art of flying; Nischoy for his part used the magic formula he had heard Dakini utter when she carried him on her back to bring him to Pushkar. "You see, my dear," Nischoy told Nanda, "there is some fun in being an actor. One acquires the art of remembering things and profits from it."

"I wish," Nanda said, "I had the good sense to teach you the Yaksha spell for flying when we exchanged our rings. That would have shortened our separation and trials."

"Now that we are joined together for good we shall forget the past and make up for the lost time."

All this happened long, long ago. But in Ujjain they still say, "Nanda and Nischoy were the most well-matched couple that ever appeared on the stage. They were also the most happily married couple."

DEBJANI CHATTERJEE

The Elephant-Headed God

HINDUS worship many gods and goddesses who are all different aspects of the one God. Ganesh is an important god in many ways. He is very near and dear to mankind, whom he is always helping. He is the "Remover of Obstacles" — so when Hindus have problems or difficulties, big or small, they turn to him. He brings good luck to his worshippers, and many Indian merchants and shopkeepers keep pictures or little carved images of him in the home, the office or even the car! But Ganesh is, above all, the god of wisdom.

Wisdom? Well, why not? That elephant head has something to do with it. He only became the god of wisdom, you see, after he acquired the elephant head. Hindus have always loved their elephants for their hard work, loyalty and gentleness. But they also respect the elephant for its great wisdom, long memory and dignity. With its wisdom and its strength the elephant is more truly the king of the animal world than any lion can be.

To learn the secret of how Ganesh got his elephant's head, I must tell you something about his parents. I am sure you will agree that it is the strangest tale of all!

Ganesh belongs to the most popular family of gods in Hinduism. He is the elder son of Parvati and Shiva. Parvati is the daughter of the Himalayas, that snowy chain of mountains that covers the north of India. She is the most beautiful and gracious goddess, a loving mother and devoted wife. Shiva — well, even his best friends will admit that he is not exactly an ideal father or husband. Shiva loves his family dearly, in his own way. It's just that he cannot bear to stay at home all the time. He has a wanderlust in him and likes to go travelling on his pet bull. Unfortunately, the places he is really keen on are remote and dangerous mountains and icy peaks — not the sort of places one takes one's family for a picnic! Shiva likes the peace of cremation grounds too. But his great passion is yoga-meditation. He cannot get enough of it and, when absorbed in meditation, even an earthquake does not disturb him. Shiva has other strange habits too. He dislikes wearing a lot of clothes, and is happiest wandering about barefoot with only a tiger skin around his waist. Naturally many gods think that he is quite mad, and everyone thought that Parvati too must have lost her senses when she married him.

For some time after his marriage Shiva was supremely happy, living with Parvati in a little cottage on Mount Kailas in the Himalayas, far away from human civilisation and also far from Indra's glittering court in heaven and all other disturbances. But after a while Parvati could see that her husband was getting restless. He would open the window and look longingly at the high mountain peaks, and a dreamy look would come into his eyes. Because she loved him deeply, Parvati understood his innermost wishes.

One day she said to Shiva, "Why don't you go away for a while? I know that you led a different life before we married. You used to meditate, and sometimes danced on cremation grounds along with your ghosts and banshee friends. You must be missing all that now."

"No, dear one," assured her husband. "My wild days are over. I really don't need them now."

"But don't you miss your companions?" she persisted.

"When I look at you, I don't notice their absence!" Shiva smiled at her mischievously. "The truth is that the ghosts, demons and banshees are all around the house, for they are never far from me. I did not wish to frighten you, so I ordered them to be invisible and to keep very quiet; and how well they have obeyed me!"

Parvati was torn between alarm and laughter — alarm at the thought of being surrounded by creatures from a nightmare world, and laughter at

Shiva's absurd pride in his friends. Shiva pleaded, "You won't ask me to send them away, will you? They are like little children, naughty at times, but they mean no harm. Why, they all love you already, for they know that you are my wife. And I know that you could not be cruel to anyone."

Parvati agreed that Shiva's companions could stay.

"What about your meditation, then?" she asked. "That used to be your main occupation. You are the greatest yogi among the gods. But even you must keep in practice. And your bull, Nandi, hasn't had any exercise for ages!"

Shiva knew that she was right. He longed to be absorbed once more in the joy of meditation, and he truly missed all his favourite mountain spots where he sat and meditated. It was, after all, his mastery of yoga that had made him a god of such great power. But still he hesitated.

"Will you not be lonely if I go?" he asked. "There is no one here but the demons, and they will follow me if I go."

Parvati assured him that she would be perfectly happy on her own. She wanted to transform their cottage, which was really no more than a bare hovel, into a comfortable and lovely place to raise a family — a real home.

So a happy Shiva stripped to his tiger skin, wrapped his favourite snakes about him, and shouted to Nandi who came galloping to his master. Waving goodbye, Shiva set off on his bull, with his weird assortment of friends.

"I won't be long," he told Parvati.

Parvati, appealing to all the ghosts, said, "Guard my husband well!"

But Shiva is a most forgetful god. And when he is meditating it is virtually impossible to rouse him. High above the sacred river Ganges, at Gangotri, Shiva sat and meditated. Many years passed, which were thousands of human years — for time is different for gods and men. When at last Shiva rose from his lotus pose, he remembered his wife waiting patiently at home on Mount Kailas, and hurriedly made his way back to her.

In the meantime Parvati had planted a lovely garden around the cottage, sewn curtains for the windows, cushions for the floor, and painted the doors and walls. She was not alone for very long, either. Shiva did not know that he had left his wife pregnant. In time Parvati had a handsome baby boy who kept her very busy indeed. She named him Ganesh. The years passed and the baby god grew into a quiet thoughtful little boy who was very attached to his mother and loved to help her in any way. He often asked Parvati about his father, and she told him that Shiva was one of the greatest of the gods, far greater than Indra who was the king of heaven.

One spring morning Parvati was enjoying a bath, while her son stood by the garden gate. A tall stranger with long matted hair, snakes wriggling about him, and wearing only an animal skin, strode up to the gate. Nandi, the bull, followed behind, for the stranger was of course none other than Shiva. He had rushed home without bothering to tidy up his wild appearance.

Shiva hesitated as he looked at the sun-bathed cottage with flowering creepers and bushes and sweet smelling herbs around it. Was this beautiful home really his? And who was the handsome boy who blocked his way?

"Let me pass, boy," said Shiva gruffly, for he was impatient to see his dear wife again.

"No," said Ganesh, frowning at the dirty vagabond trying to force his way in. "You may not enter."

But brushing the boy aside, Shiva walked straight through the garden to the house. Ganesh knew that his mother was bathing inside the cottage, and that this rude fellow must be prevented at all cost from entering. He rushed to the door and drew out his sword. Poor boy! What a moment to rouse his father's anger. Shiva is the most quick-tempered god, though he is quick to forgive as well. Now he lost his temper completely. Shiva's third eye of power blazed fire from the middle of his forehead, and in seconds a headless and helpless body was all that lay between him and the cottage door.

On hearing voices, Parvati had quickly stepped out of the bath. She opened the door, only to find her son without a head and the long-absent husband eager to embrace her. She tore herself from his arms and wept bitterly. Nandi, the bull, whimpered in sympathy.

"What have you done? What have you done?" she repeated, wringing her hands. "That is our son whom you have destroyed!" Her grief was dreadful to see.

Shiva was truly sorry now. He tried to comfort her. "Our son is a god, so he is not dead. He is only stunned for a while. I haven't destroyed him, only his head. He does not really need a head to be himself."

But Parvati would have none of it. "You have destroyed him, crazy yogi that you are! What use is a god without a head?"

Shiva tried his best to convince her that no great harm had been done. After all, he had once destroyed the entire body of Kama, the god of Love. And everyone knows what an active god Kama is. He does not need a body to roam through the universe, shooting his arrows. But Parvati insisted that Shiva restore Ganesh's head.

"But I can't undo what I've already done!" Shiva protested.

It was no use. He felt desperate. He simply could not bear to listen to Parvati weeping.

At length Shiva promised to bring back the head of the first sleeper he met who was lying in the "wrong position". Hindus believe that it is best to sleep along the earth's magnetic line, with the head towards the North Pole and the feet pointing towards the South Pole. Someone sleeping in the "wrong position" would, therefore, do just the opposite, and have his or her head towards the south and feet towards the north.

After searching for several miles, Shiva came across a baby elephant that was sleeping in the wrong position. Shiva had already given his word. He had not said that he would bring back the first boy's head, or even a human head, so now it was the baby elephant's head he removed. Shiva quickly returned to the cottage with the elephant head and placed it on his son's shoulders.

A baby's head is very big and heavy, especially when it is that of a baby elephant. So Ganesh found it difficult to balance his new head at first, with its long wriggly trunk and large fan-like ears. Parvati was horrified to see Ganesh's new head. Shiva really must be mad, she thought. Her poor son! He would surely become the laughing stock of heaven! She decided to ask help of the other gods and goddesses, on behalf of Ganesh.

Parvati lifted her son in her arms and flew up with him, straight to heaven. She did not stop till she found herself in Indra's court. A hush came over all the gods and goddesses when they saw a weeping Parvati carrying a strange little boy with an elephant head. Indra and his queen rose from their golden thrones to greet Parvati.

"Gracious goddess," said the king of heaven, "we have sadly missed you since your marriage. And now you come to us with tears in your beautiful eyes. You have only to command us. In what way may we help you?" Other gods and goddesses too came crowding around Parvati, for she is much loved in heaven and on earth.

Parvati told them about Ganesh's accident and begged Indra to give Ganesh a proper head instead.

"I do understand how you feel, Parvati," said Indra. "But what you suggest is impossible. I am king of all the lesser gods and goddesses. But Shiva and you are far greater than I. There is nothing that I can do which is not in your power to do as well.

If Shiva has given your son an elephant head, it must be what is best for the boy."

Shachi, the queen of heaven, had a suggestion. It was true that no god or goddess was greater than Shiva, and Parvati who was his equal was too unhappy to think calmly about what was best for Ganesh, but Shachi reminded them that there were two other gods who were also Shiva's equals in power. They were Brahma the Creator, and Vishnu the Preserver. Hindus believe that Brahma, Vishnu and Shiva are three equal aspects of God.

No sooner did Shachi mention their names than the two great gods appeared.

"My brother gods, have pity on my innocent son," pleaded Parvati. "Must he suffer like this for his father's quick temper and madness?"

Both the gods asked Parvati to dry her tears, for all would be well. Brahma, who loves children, sat on Indra's throne and seated Ganesh on his knee. Vishnu smiled at Parvati and asked her to forgive her husband. "Shiva did not know what he was doing when his third eye burnt away Ganesh's head. But your son has lost nothing by it. He is lucky to be the son of Shiva and Parvati, and he will become a great god in his own right. He may not be a handsome god any more, but all will recognise his goodness and love him for himself. Alone among the gods and goddesses, he has an elephant head, so he will never be forgotten or ignored and will have a special place in heaven and in the hearts of people."

Actually, Brahma thought the elephant head was rather attractive. Both Brahma and Vishnu showered their blessings on the boy and gave him special gifts.

"Ganesh with his elephant head will be the god of wisdom," said Brahma. "Writers will worship him. He will be the scribe of heaven, and the god of literature."

"He will be the remover of obstacles," added Vishnu, "and will be worshipped first at any religious ceremony, before any other gods are worshipped. He is the god who will smile good fortune on any new undertaking."

Parvati felt much happier now, even though Ganesh still had an elephant head. She warmly thanked all the gods and goddesses.

Shiva was waiting at the cottage on Mount Kailas. He knew what was happening at Indra's court, for he could see it all with his magical third eye. When Parvati returned with their son, Shiva lovingly welcomed them.

To this day, Ganesh lives happily with his parents. He also lives in the hearts of his worshippers. He is now a plump god who can easily support his elephant head. All religious festivals for Hindus begin with his worship and many books by Hindus have, at the beginning, a prayer to the elephant-headed god of wisdom.

Brahma and Vishnu were right. The elephant-headed god is much loved by Hindus. Hindus also love to tell, and listen to the many stories about Ganesh's kindness and friendliness, his love of food, and his wisdom.

As well as being the god of wisdom, Ganesh was also made the scribe of heaven. When Indra, the king of heaven, has any important proclamation to be written down, when some god wants a letter written to a shy goddess, or when the twin gods of medicine have a lengthy prescription to write, they all ask Ganesh to help, for he has the most beautiful handwriting, is exceptionally good at spelling, and can write astonishingly fast — almost at the speed of thought! Oh, one other thing. I did not mention the fact that his is no ordinary pen. In his chubby right hand Ganesh holds part of an ivory elephant tusk which he dips in ink and writes with! There is an interesting story behind this.

It happened in this way. Thousands of years ago, the wise sage Vyasa wanted to compose a long and beautiful poem to tell the history of his people and teach them to live noble lives. But it would be such a long poem that Vyasa feared he might not live to finish writing it, for he was an old man. In his difficulty, Vyasa prayed to Ganesh.

"You are the scribe of the gods, Ganesh," the old man prayed, "but will you work for me, for a change? If you do not write down my dictation my work will be lost to the world. But I am poor and have nothing to pay you with. Indeed, what can one offer a god for such a service? You must work for the joy of listening to my words alone."

You might think that Ganesh would have had enough on his hands without coming and slaving away for weeks and perhaps months for an old man whose poem would probably turn out to be dreadfully boring anyway, especially if it was going to be full of history and teachings. But Ganesh is a most generous god. He was sorry for the old sage and wanted to help him, even though he had his doubts about how good his poem might be.

The god agreed to help Vyasa on one condition.

"Once you start dictating you must not stop till you come to the end. I will write down your words as fast as you recite them. But if at any time you pause for thought or rest, I shall get bored and stop writing immediately. I'm afraid your work will then remain incomplete."

The old man was overjoyed to have the god of wisdom working as his scribe. Afraid to delay even for a moment in case Ganesh got bored before he started, or changed his mind, Vyasa hurriedly started reciting his poem. A little taken aback at such speed, Ganesh glanced about him for something to write with. He had not come prepared with a pen. But the words of the old poet were ringing in his elephant head, and they were of marvellous power and beauty. Anxious not to lose a single word from the wise Vyasa's lips, and completely forgetting everything except for his need to write down the poem, Ganesh broke off half of his left tusk and dipped it in ink.

The result of this extraordinary partnership of man and god is the longest poem in the world — it has about 180,000 lines — and one of the best. It is called the *Mahabharata*, which means "The Great Story of India". You may like to read it yourself one day.

Do you remember the rat mentioned at the beginning of this story the rat who is always in pictures of Ganesh? He was once a proud and wicked monster. Frightened people prayed to Ganesh to save them from this terrible giant. When Ganesh told the monster to stop bullying people, he simply laughed, for he did not believe that Ganesh could stop him. So the god lifted one foot, and squashing the giant to the ground, turned him into a lowly rat. But Ganesh is so kindhearted that he would not abandon the mon- ster after he had become a little rat. Besides, the monster was now sorry that he had been so wicked and promised to turn over a new leaf. Ganesh, therefore, decided to keep the rat near him always as his pet.

The Hindu gods and goddesses have special animals to ride upon. Shiva's pet, of course, is Nandi the bull. Indra rides upon a white elephant. The goddess Durga rides a tiger. So the rat became Ganesh's pet; and you may not believe it, but Ganesh rides upon the rat whenever he has to go anywhere! You see, for a god — especially such an unusual god as Ganesh — all things are possible.

DEBJANI CHATTERJEE

Krishna — Man and God

KRISHNA was the noble king of Dwarka nearly four thousand years ago. He was famous for his wisdom — a philosopher-king they called him. He ruled with both justice and mercy. Many people sought his advice and he never turned away a single person who sincerely asked for his help. For all his royal dignity and many kingly accomplishments, Krishna always remembered his humble upbringing in the forest of Brindaban where, as a boy he had looked after his foster parents' cattle and played with the other cow-herds. Although he now wore a golden crown, he still sported a peacock feather in his curly black hair to remind him of those carefree days, and was known on occasions to put away his rich clothes and become again the simple fun-loving youth when his childhood friends called on him. Krishna was, in fact, the great god Vishnu, born on earth just as he had been born many times before — for special purposes.

Naturally Krishna was very popular. Even people who did not get along with each other would still be proud to count him as a mutual friend. The Pandava princes, for instance, who were the five sons of King Pandu, became good friends of Krishna. Closest to him, among them, was the third brother, Arjuna, said to be the finest archer in all the world. But Krishna was friendly too with their cousins and sworn enemies, the hundred Kaurava brothers whose greed for more power and territory had led them to make many attempts on the lives of their five cousins. Through trickery and deceit, the Kauravas succeeded more than once in having the Pandavas banished to the forests for several years while they seized the whole kingdom for themselves.

You may be sure that the five princes had many strange adventures while they were exiled in the forest. One of the most wonderful of these was how they came to win the hand in marriage of the beautiful princess Draupadi. Yes, one wife for five brothers! It was in the process of winning Draupadi during their first exile that the Pandavas met Krishna, and it was the start of a lifelong friendship.

In ancient India it was the custom for highborn ladies to choose their own husbands at a special ceremony where all their suitors would be present. To help them make their choice the suitors were often set difficult or dangerous tasks so that they could prove their worth. The eventual winner would then hope to marry the princess whose ceremony it was.

Draupadi, daughter of King Drupada of Panchala, was as virtuous as she was beautiful. She had great strength of character too, and from her childhood had worshipped God with great devotion. When it was time for her to choose a husband, her father issued invitations far and wide for suitors to come to a ceremony and prove themselves worthy to marry his daughter. Many were the princes who were eager to win Draupadi as a bride. Among them was Duryodhana, the eldest of the Kaurava brothers, and also, disguised as beggars, were the five Pandava brothers. Sitting among the family guests with King Drupada and his lovely daughter was Krishna, the king of Dwarka.

The task set seemed impossible to most of the suitors. They were handed a great bow and asked to string it and shoot five arrows through the hole in a revolving disk at a tiny target shaped like a fish, which they could only see as a reflection in the water of a well. One by one the distinguished suitors tried, but walked away defeated. Most of them could not even bend the mighty bow, let alone string it. To fail like this was a great blow to Duryodhana's pride.

"No human can perform this task!" he complained. "At this rate the lady will have none left to marry her."

Arjuna now stepped forward to lift the bow, but was met with an outcry. Duryodhana and his friends did not think it right that a beggar should enter the contest. But Draupadi had noticed that the five beggars were handsome men whose ragged clothes did not hide their heroic build. She willingly gave her agreement for Arjuna to take part in the contest. Nor was Krishna fooled. As soon as he saw the five beggars he guessed that these must be the princes in exile, disguised to avoid detection by Duryodhana and his spies, for the story of the five Pandava brothers who had lost their kingdom and wandered in the forest was well-known.

Krishna spoke softly to pacify some of the angry suitors. "Since the fair Draupadi agrees, let this man be put to the test, gentle princes, kings and friends. A man's true nature proclaims whether he is a prince or a beggar. Do not judge anyone by outward appearances."

Arjuna looked into the kindly eyes of the king of Dwarka and sent him a silent message of thanks. Then, with a prayer to Vishnu in his heart, he picked up the giant bow, bent it and easily placed the string on it. As the crowd gasped in amazement, for no one had so far succeeded in stringing the bow, Arjuna fitted an arrow to the string, lifted the bow above his head and looking steadfastly at the reflection in the well water he let fly at the target. His arrow winged its way through the tiny hole in the revolving disk and hit the fish hanging high above. Without stopping Arjuna shot another arrow and then another, till all five arrows had hit their target and the bright metal fish fell to the ground.

Arjuna's triumph was complete when Draupadi put her flower garland around his neck and chose him as her husband. So at the end of the day it was the beggar-prince, accompanied by his four brothers, who led away the famous princes, while Duryodhana returned to his own capital city of Hastinapura in disgust.

The Pandava princes were in the habit of sharing everything with each other. Living in the forest as they did, with their widowed mother, Kunti, they all depended on Arjuna's skill with bow and arrow to obtain their food. Sometimes it was venison and sometimes a rabbit. On this day when Arjuna called out to his mother to see what prize his archery had brought home, Kunti did not turn around to look. Instead, she said, with an absent-minded air, "Oh good! Of course you will share with your brothers, as usual!"

Now, a mother's word is a command for a dutiful son. Draupadi and the Pandava brothers were horrified, as was Kunti herself when she realised what she had said, but they all knew that they were now bound by honour to share Draupadi as their common wife. At this moment Krishna appeared. He had secretly followed them to the cottage deep in the forest.

"Do not worry, daughter," he comforted the princess. "It is your destiny to have the five noblest men any girl would like to have as husbands. You are the most fortunate of women. Your happiness in marriage will be multiplied five times! I know that you will be able to manage this situation."

With a mischievous smile the laughter-loving Krishna showed Draupadi his divine form. "Do you remember your daily prayer to me, these many years? It was: 'Lord, may I marry the noblest man in all the world.' You repeated it five times each day. Princess, your prayer is granted."

Draupadi trembled to see the shining gracious form of the beloved Vishnu of her prayers.

This was a great spiritual moment. Vishnu, she now knew, was on earth as the philosopher-king, Krishna.

Krishna blessed Draupadi and Kunti and her sons, promising them his protection in the difficult times to come.

Krishna's prophecy came true. So greatly did the brothers love and respect one another and Draupadi, their queen, that this unusual marriage worked perfectly. They all lived together in peace and joy.

But hard times were soon upon them. When the years of their exile ended, the Pandava brothers returned to their kingdom. But the evil Duryodhana drove them out once again. He even dared to do a most insulting thing. He sent one of this younger brothers to fetch Draupadi to his court. The Kaurava prince dragged the unwilling lady by her beautiful long hair, until she stood in the palace court of Hastinapura surrounded by the jeering kauravas. Wishing to humiliate his Pandava cousins through their queen, the eldest of the Kaurava brothers gave the order for her to be disrobed. Rough hands pulled at Draupadi's sari.

Draupadi stood tall and proud in her grief and anger. She closed her eyes and called upon Krishna to rescue her honour. Everyone present at the court of Hastinapura witnessed a miracle that day. Round and round the lady turned and metre upon metre of shimmering silk sari cascaded onto the marble floor. It seemed as if Draupadi wore a never-endings sari, and all present rubbed their eyes as one colourful sari seemed to merge with yet another. Draupadi alone with closed eyes could see the beautiful form of Vishnu in the hall. She remembered how, in her childhood play as she dressed her dolls in saris, she had always thought of him. "Here are those same saris now," said the god, "increased many times over. Such is the power of prayer."

Finding that they were unable to disrobe Draupadi, the Kauravas gave up their shameful attempt.

Driven out by their cousins for the second time, the Pandavas went into exile for thirteen

years, accompanied by Draupadi. Once more
they lived a simple life in the forest where many
gods, demons, and wise men came their way. But
they were not forgotten by their own world either, for their powerful friend, Krishna, the king
of Dwarka, would sometimes visit them. They
developed great faith in Krishna and trusted him
to guide their lives in all matters.

When the long years of their second exile finally ended, then Pandavas found the Kauravas
once again unwilling to return their kingdom to
them. Krishna himself acted as a go-between and
pleaded for the five brothers. He reminded
Duryodhana that he had made a solemn promise,
in public, to restore the kingdom to the Pandavas
at the end of thirteen years. But the Kaurava
prince was not a man of honour and did not
hesitate to break his word. Krishna knew that war
would break out between the cousins if the
Pandavas continued to be cheated of their inher-
itance, and that many thousands would die. In the
cause of peace, and to give the Kauravas every
chance to undo their wrong, Krishna made one
last effort.

"Duryodhana, if you will not return them half the kingdom along with the beautiful city of Indraprastha which your cousins built from the wilderness, at least give them five villages to rule over."

But the greedy Kauravas refused to accept even this.

War was inevitable. The Pandavas knew that they had to fight for their kingdom even if they died in the attempt. Many were the kings and nobles who came to ally themselves with the Pandavas in order to help them in their just cause. But many who were friends and relatives of both sides, felt painfully divided in their loyalty. Some simply gave their support to whichever side was the first to ask for it. This was the case for instance with Drona, the warrior and teacher of both the Pandavas and the Kauravas in their youth. Drona had always tried to treat the princes in his charge with equal fairness. He had watched them growing up together: Yudhishtira the just, eldest of the sons of king Pandu, who showed all the early signs of becoming a great king; Bhima the strong, the second Pandava, who was a giant of a man; and Arjuna, that prince among archers who had become Drona's favourite pupil. Yet it was Duryodhana who first requested Drona's help in the great war to come and Drona agreed to become one of the Kaurava captains.

Duryodhana, on behalf of the Kauravas, and Arjuna, on behalf on the Pandavas, came to ask Krishna for help. Duryodhana arrived first and was told by servants that their royal master was asleep. But he was not going to risk losing Krishna's help, so he entered the bedroom and sat down in a grand throne-like chair by Krishna's head. When Arjuna arrived he learnt that his cousin was waiting in the bedroom for Krishna to wake up, so he too went to the bedroom but sat down more humbly at the foot of Krishna's bed. When the king of Dwarka awoke he was glad to see Arjuna, for it was the Pandava prince that he saw first.

But Duryodhana quickly pressed his claim: "I was here first and so surely it is I who should have your help!"

Speaking very calmly Krishna said that both had equal claims to seek his help, Arjuna whom he had seen first, and Duryodhana who had arrived first. "You must choose," he said, "the kind of help you want. On the one hand there is my vast army of trained soldiers with weapons, horses, and elephants. On the other hand there is only myself. If one of you should choose me I will help you, but I shall not myself use any weapon in the war to come."

The two cousins quickly made up their minds, each according to his nature. For Duryodhana it was obvious that the powerful army was worth having on his side in the battles to come, an unarmed Krishna could in no way match so powerful a force. Arjuna was equally sure that nothing in the world mattered except that God should be on his side. There were moments when the pure-hearted prince recognised that Krishna was really God, and in his mercy he appeared to Arjuna as a loving human friend and wise counsellor. How it came to be that Krishna was both God and man, Arjuna did not stop to puzzle.

"Krishna, you are all that I want," said the Pandava hero.

"So be it," declared Krishna, and the two cousins left him, each feeling well-satisfied.

True to his promise, Krishna sent his army, fully equipped, to swell the numbers of the Kaurava force, while he himself, carrying no weapons, became Arjuna's charioteer.

On the battlefield of Kurukshetra the two armies faced each other, and before the battle began Arjuna looked across to the opposite side where he saw many friends and relatives, people he loved and admired, now ranged against him. A terrible sorrow overcame him and he felt that he could not wage war on such men as these. If he won, it would only be by killing those he held dear, people such as his beloved teacher Drona, and such a victory would not be worth having.

Krishna realised the confusion and doubt that gripped Arjuna's mind. Now more than ever did Arjuna need the guidance of his friend, the philosopher-king. Luckily Krishna's words of wisdom at this critical time have come down to us as the *Bhagavad Gita*, which means the "Song of God". In eloquent words Krishna reminded his friend of where his duty lay.

"Man must do his duty without thinking of any reward," taught Krishna.

Arjuna understood that his duty as a prince lay in fighting evil, not because he hoped to win, but because evil must never be tolerated. He learnt that man was more than just a body, he was also a soul which could never die. Arjuna also discovered that Krishna had, like him, been born to fulfil a special purpose.

"Age after age I am born on this earth, to protect the good and to destroy the evildoer. Whenever the conditions call for my presence in the world, then I am born to carry out my mission," was the gracious promise of Krishna.

While the two armies waited, still and tense, as though frozen in time, Arjuna had a glimpse of Krishna's true nature. Where a moment ago stood his trusted charioteer, Arjuna now saw the mind-shattering form of God as master of the universe. The two great armies, the battlefield, he himself, the universe, nothing existed except God. Awestruck by this mighty vision the Pandava hero turned away his face.

"Lord, protect me!" he cried. "Show me once more the human form of my charioteer and friend."

The smiling face of Krishna appeared before him again, a peacock feather in his dark hair. His moment of rare knowledge had brought Arjuna very close to God, and now with renewed strength of purpose he lifted his famous bow, Gandiva, to challenge the enemy.

For eighteen days the battle raged and the field of Kurukshetra ran red with blood. Few were left alive on either side. Krishna had foreseen this terrible destruction and had cast his protection over the Pandava brothers, all of whom survived the war and won for Yudhishtira, the eldest of them, the combined kingdom of the Kauravas and the Pandavas.

One other family survived the slaughter, thanks to the mercy of God. A little lapwing had built a nest of grass and twigs right in the middle of the battlefield. The nest with its tiny eggs lay hidden in the taller grass but once the battle began it seemed certain that it would be trampled under the feet of soldiers, horses, and elephants, or crushed beneath chariot wheels. But even when the war conches blew, and the earth shook as the armies prepared to fight, the little bird refused to leave her nest helpless and unprotected. Her tiny despairing cries were heard by Krishna who left his chariot and followed the sound until he found the lapwing and her nest.

"Little mother," he said in his gentle voice, "your devotion to your family is the highest form of love. You and your innocent little ones have no part in this terrible war. You will not suffer because of it."

Krishna blessed the bird and her still unhatched brood. Then he picked up an elephant bell that had fallen on the battlefield. These large bronze bells were proudly worn on a chain round the necks of war elephants in ancient India. Very carefully Krishna covered the lapwing and her nest with the great bell. In this way they were kept safe for the whole of that fearsome battle.

Thousands of years have passed since these events took place. The modern city of Meerut now stands where the Kauravas once had their capital city, Hastinapura. Over the ruins of the proud Pandava city of Indraprastha flies the national flag of India, for this site is now Delhi, the country's historic capital. The field of Kurukshetra lies still and bare with only the wind blowing through the tall grass, but if you listen carefully you may just hear the happy song of the lapwings drifting on the breeze. The noble deeds of the Pandavas live on in the memory, and the inspiring song of Krishna uplifts the hearts of men. God's mercy continues to protect the world, even the tiniest bird.

RUSKIN BOND

Shakuntala

IN ANCIENT INDIA, when the great God Indra was worshipped, there lived a young king named Dushyanta.

One day, while he was hunting in a great forest, the king became separated from his followers. He wandered on alone through the forest until he found himself in a pleasant grove which led to a hermitage. The little dwelling was the home of an old hermit called Father Kanva. The king had heard many stories about the piety and wisdom of the old man, and decided to honour him with a visit.

To the king's disappointment, however, the hermitage was empty. He turned away and was about to leave the grove when a gentle voice said, "Wait, my lord," and a girl stepped out from behind the trees.

In spite of her poor clothes, the girl was so beautiful and dignified that the king's admiration was aroused and he asked her courteously, "Isn't this the dwelling place of holy Kanva?"

"Yes, my lord," she replied. "But my father is away on a pilgrimage. Will you not rest here a while?"

She brought him water and fruits for his refreshment, and the king was delighted at the hospitality he was shown. It was clear to him that she did not recognise him as the king: so Dushyanta, who liked to mingle unrecognised among his people, pretended to be a huntsman, and asked the girl her name.

"I am called Shakuntala," she said. "I am Father Kanva's adopted daughter."

Encouraged to go on, she told the king that

she had been left an orphan when she was very small, and that Kanva had treated her as lovingly as if he had really been her father. Though she was of noble birth, she was very happy living a simple life in the forest.

As Dushyanta listened to her and watched her beautiful face, he felt that he could linger in that enchanting spot for ever; but he knew that his followers must be anxiously searching for him, so he took leave of Shakuntala and made his way back to the hunting party.

But he did not leave the forest. Instead he ordered his men to encamp at some distance from the hermitage. The next day, and the following day as well, found him visiting Shakuntala at the hermitage.

Dushyanta and Shakuntala were soon confessing their love for each other; but when the girl learnt that it was the king himself who wished to marry her, she protested that he would surely regret such a hasty decision. Dushyanta, however, soothed her fears, and, dreading lest something might come between them, persuaded her to wed him without delay.

There was no need for a priest to marry the lovers, since, in those days it was lawful for kings and warriors to wed their brides by a simple exchange of flowers or garlands. And so Dushyanta and Shakuntala vowed to be true to each other for ever.

"Come with me to my palace," said the king. "My people shall acknowledge you as their queen."

"I cannot leave the forest until I have told Father Kanva of our marriage," said Shakuntala. "I must wait for him to return. But you must return to your palace to carry out your duties. When you come again, I will be ready to join you."

The king placed a ring, engraven with the name "Dushyanta", upon her finger, and promised to return soon.

When he had left, Shakuntala wandered dreamily about the forest, forgetting that someone might visit the hermitage to see Father Kanva. At nightfall when she returned to the grove, she was met by a visitor who was spluttering with rage.

The visitor was an old sage named Durvasas, who was dreaded by all because of his violent temper. It was said that if anyone offended him, he would punish them severely. He was known as a "master-curser".

The sage had been waiting at the hermitage for a long time, and felt that he had been insulted by Shakuntala. She pleaded for forgiveness, and begged him to stay; but the old man was in a terrible mood. Thrusting the girl aside, he hurried away muttering a curse under his breath.

Shakuntala was troubled not so much by the curse as by the feeling that she had neglected her duties; for in India it is something of a sin if one receives a visitor and allows the guest to depart unhonoured.

Then something happened which worried Shakuntala even more. Whilst she was bathing in the stream near her home, the ring, the king's gift, slipped from her finger and disappeared in the water.

Shakuntala wept bitterly at her loss; but she was not to know what heartbreak it was to bring her in the future, or how closely her bad luck was connected with the angry sage Durvasas.

It was a great relief to her when Father Kanva returned from his pilgrimage. He was not displeased at the news of her marriage to Dushyanta. On the contrary, he was overjoyed.

"My daughter, you are worthy of the king," he said. "Gladly will I give you to Dushyanta when he comes to claim you."

But the days passed, and King Dushyanta did not come.

Shakuntala felt a great weight begin to press against her heart. What could have happened? Was Dushyanta ill, or was he repentant of his rash marriage? But no, she could never believe that...

Then Father Kanva, growing uneasy, said: "My daughter, since the king has not come, you must seek him at his palace. For though it grieves me to part with you, a wife's place is by her husband's side."

Dushyanta had asked her to wait for him; but she could not refuse to do Father Kanva's bidding. And so, for the first time in her life, she left her forest home and journeyed to the unknown world beyond.

After several days she reached the royal city, and, learning that the king was in his palace, she asked permission to see him, saying that she had brought a message from Father Kanva.

When she found herself at the foot of the king's throne, she looked up so that he could see her face, and said, "Do not be angry with me, my lord, but since you did not keep your promise to claim me soon, I have been forced to seek you here."

"My promise to claim you?" King Dushyanta looked bewildered. "What do you mean?"

Shakuntala looked at him with fear in her eyes.

"You are mocking me, my lord," she said. "Have you forgotten our marriage in the forest, and how you said you would cherish me for ever? Do not look so strangely at me, I beg you, but acknowledge me as your bride!"

"My bride!" exclaimed the king. "What fantasy is this? I have never seen you before!"

Shakuntala was astounded. What has happened to him? she wondered. I have always dreaded that he would repent our hasty marriage. But surely he would not deny me? And she stretched out her arms to him and cried, "How can you say such words? They are not worthy of a king. What have I done that you should treat me so cruelly?"

"I have never seen you before," said the king firmly. "You must be either mad or wicked to come to me with such a tale."

Shakuntala stood looking at him with growing despair in her heart. Then, realising from the king's hard countenance the hopelessness of her situation, she fled from the palace, weeping bitterly.

Now, although King Dushyanta appeared to have become callous and cruel in such a short space of time, in reality he had only spoken what he believed to be the truth. He did not remember Shakuntala at all, and for a very good reason. When the old sage Durvasas had muttered his curse, he had decreed, first of all, that she should lose the king's ring, and then, that until Dushayant saw the ring again, he would be unable to remember Shakuntala, even though she stood before him.

Not even God Indra could alter a curse once it had been pronounced by the old sage, and since Dushyanta's ring had been swept away by the stream in the forest, there was little hope that he would ever remember his bride.

Several years passed, and then one day a fisherman was brought before the king to relate a curious story.

The fisherman had caught a fine carp in the river, and when he had cut the fish open a gold ring engraven with the name "Dushyanta" was found within the body of the carp.

The king examined the ring with interest. "It does look like mine," he said, "yet I don't remember losing it."

He rewarded the fisherman for his honesty, and after examining the ring again, he placed it upon his finger.

"How strange!" he said. "A cloud seems to be lifting from my mind. Yes, I remember now — this is the ring I gave to my bride, Shakuntala, in the forest. Ah, but what have I done! It was Shakuntala who came to me that day, and I sent her away with cruel words."

Dushyanta hastened to the forest, but the hermitage was deserted. Father Kanva was long since dead. The king had the land searched, but it was as though Shakuntala had vanished from the earth. He fell into a deep melancholy from which no one could rouse him.

But although God Indra had not been able to avert the curse of Durvasas, he had not been indifferent to the suffering that had been caused. And now that the ring had been recovered, he was determined to help the unhappy king.

One day Dushyanta was walking in his garden when he saw a strange object in the sky. It looked like a great shining bird.

As it came nearer, the bird proved to be a chariot drawn by prancing horses, whose reins were held by a celestial-looking being.

The chariot alighted on the earth not far from the king, and the charioteer called: "Dushyanta! Do you not know me? I am Matali, the charioteer of great Indra. Come with me, for Indra has need of you."

Dushyanta was awestruck; but he stepped into the chariot and was whirled upwards so swiftly that soon his kingdom lay like a speck beneath him. The chariot soared still higher, and the horses trod the air as if it were solid ground beneath their feet. Then suddenly the chariot stopped in the midst of the clouds, and Matali told Dushyanta to descent.

The king obeyed, and gradually, as the mist cleared and the clouds melted away, he saw that he was alone in a beautiful garden. He felt that surely he was near great Indra's dwelling.

There was a rustling in the bushes, and Dushyanta waited breathlessly. Perhaps God was about to reveal himself.

It was not a heavenly being who appeared, however, but a little boy who was carrying a lion cub. The cub struggled fiercely in his arms, but the boy held on to it without fear.

"Come here, boy," called the king. "Tell me your name."

"I do not know it," said the boy.

"That is strange," said Dushyanta. He felt irresistibly drawn towards the boy, and held out his hand to him, but the boy drew back.

"No one shall touch me," he said, and then called out: "Mother, come quickly!"

"I am coming, son," said a gentle voice.

The king stepped back, trembling violently, for there before him stood Shakuntala, looking pale and sad but more beautiful than ever.

When she saw the king she drew herself up proudly, but Dushyanta fell at her feet, crying: "Shakuntala, do not turn away from me. Listen, I beg of you!" And he told her of how he had forgotten her until the recovery of the ring, and of how he had since sought her everywhere.

Shakuntala's face lit up with joy and she cried, "Oh, Dushyanta, now I understand. It must have been the punishment of Durvasas." And she told him about the curse of the angry sage, how she had lost her ring in the stream, and how she had suffered all these years at the thought of her husband's denial of her.

"But where have you been all this time?" asked Dushyanta. "What place is this?"

"This is a sacred mountain near the dwelling place of great Indra. When you denied me in your palace, I felt that I should die of grief. But a wonderful thing happened to me. As I lay weeping on the ground, Indra send his chariot to earth, and I was brought here by heavenly beings who have watched over us all this time."

"Mother," cried the boy, who had been watching from a little distance. "Who is this man?"

"Your father, my child," said Shakuntala. "Embrace your son, Dushyanta. He was a gift from the gods to comfort me in my loneliness." And as Dushyanta knelt down to embrace his son, Matali again appeared in his chariot.

"Are you happy, Dushyanta?" he asked, "Now it is Indra's wish that you return with me to earth. Cherish your son, happy mortals, for he shall become the founder of a race of heroes."

The chariot took them back to earth, and from that time Dushyanta and Shakuntala lived in great happiness, while their son, whom they named Bharata, grew up to found a noble race, as Matali had foretold.

Love Conquers All

LONG LONG ago there was a king who ruled over a large part of India. He was a great horseman, and when he rode he was like a strong wind rushing by. Horses knew and loved him, and because of his power over them he was known as the Lord-of-Horses.

In spite of his fame and popularity, the king was unhappy, for no children had been born to him, and in India this was always considered a great calamity. He went from temple to temple, praying and offering sacrifices, but to no avail — it seemed as though the gods were displeased with him.

Finally, he consulted the great sage Narada.

"How can I please the gods?" he asked. "I have been married five years, but still there is no heir to the throne."

"Build a new temple," said Narada. "Build a temple to Brahma the Creator."

"I shall build the most beautiful temple in the land," said the king, and he immediately summoned his best workmen and told them to build a temple taller than any other.

"Let it be taller than three palm trees," he said. "Paint it gold without and gold within. A hundred steps of pure white marble must lead up to it."

Within a few months a beautiful golden temple was built, surrounded by flowering trees and shrubs. And every day the king visited the temple, making special offerings to Brahma, God of Creation, and his wife, Savitri, that they might send him a son.

His queen and his nobles, and even the sage Narada, had almost given up hope, when one day, as the king laid his offerings before the shrine, he thought he saw a figure growing out of the flames that had sprung up from his sacrifice. And then he heard a voice — the voice, he thought, of a goddess because though it was small and sweet it filled the temple with its sound.

"You have pleased me with your devotion," were the words he heard. "I am Savitri, wife of Brahma. What is it you seek?"

His voice trembling, the king said, "Goddess, I desire a son, so that my name may not perish from the land."

"I will give you a daughter," replied the clear sweet voice.

The fire died down and the figure faded.

And not long afterwards there was great rejoicing in the king's palace. A daughter was born to the queen — a girl so radiantly beautiful that her parents were convinced that she was heaven-born, and sent out a proclamation saying that the child was to be called "Savitri" after the wife of Brahma.

As Savitri grew up, her father began to think about her marriage, and he decided that she should choose a husband for herself from among the princes of the neighbouring states. He had no intention of imposing his will upon her.

"Daughter," he said one day, "do you wish to marry? You may, if you wish, visit the palaces of our neighbouring kings and choose a husband for yourself from among the princes. I know that you are as wise as you are lovely, and that your choice will be pleasing to me."

Savitri decided that she would seek her husband, not among her wealthy and royal neighbours, but among the remote dwellings of the hermits in the forest. She had her chariot prepared for a long journey, and ordered her drivers to take the path that led into the wilderness.

After driving through the forest for several hours, the chariot-drivers told Savitri that a hermitage lay ahead. Savitri and her handmaidens got down from the chariot and approached a small temple, beside which stood a hut made of leaves and branches. Inside the hut they found an old man who, though blind and white-haired, had an upright bearing. He was, in fact, not a priest but a king; many years ago he had gone blind and had been driven from his kingdom by a rival who took over his throne and threatened death to any of the king's family who tried to return.

As Savitri stood watching the blind old man, a youth on a black horse came riding through the forest and up to the door of the hut.

"He dresses like a peasant," said Savitri to herself "but he sits on his horse like a prince." And when she saw his face, her own lit up, for she knew that she had seen the man she would marry.

The youth dismounted, tethered his horse, greeted the old man with tender affection, and went into the hut.

"We need search no further," said Savitri to her handmaidens. "Let us ask the hospitality of these good people, and then in a few days we will return home."

The old king made them welcome. He told them of his misfortunes and of how he, and his wife, and their little son Satyavan, had been driven from the kingdom of Shalwa twenty years ago, and had lived ever since among the hermits of the forest. Satyavan stood aside, watching Savitri, and falling further in love with her every moment.

Not many days had passed before they had vowed to marry each other, but Savitri said that first she must return to her father's kingdom and obtain his consent to the marriage, after which she would come back to the forest and follow Satyavan for the rest of her life.

"But do not tell your parents as yet," she said. "Let me first speak to my father."

Savitri returned to her father's palace and found him holding counsel with Narada. The sage had suggested that it was time that a husband was found for Savitri.

"Well, here she is," said the king, as Savitri approached. "She will tell you whether or not she has found a husband."

"Yes, father, I have," she cried, as she knelt at his feet for blessing. "In his dress and his possessions he is a poor man's son, but by birth he is a prince."

"And his name?"

"Satyavan."

Before she could say another word, Narada, looking horrified, stood up and with raised hand, said: "No, Princess, not Satyavan!"

"There can be no other," said Savitri with a smile.

The king turned to Narada and asked: "Is there something wrong with the youth? Is he not all that my daughter takes him for?"

"He is all that she says ..."

"Then is he already betrothed? Is there a curse upon him?"

Narada bowed his head and in a low voice said: "He is destined for an early death. Yama, the god of death, has set his noose for him. Within a year the prince must die."

Savitri went pale, and almost fainted. But she summoned up all her courage and said, "Narada, you have prophesied his doom. I can but pray and hope. But even the knowledge of this terrible fate cannot shake my purpose. Satyavan shall be my husband for a year, even if for fifty I must be widow!"

The sage stood silent, his head sunk upon his breast. Then finally he raised his hands towards Savitri in blessing.

"Peace be with you, daughter of the Lord-of-Horses," he said, and turned and walked away.

The next day it was announced that the Princess Savitri would soon marry a prince in a distant region, and that, since the journey would be long and tedious, only her father would accompany her. Preparations were soon made, and the Lord-of-Horses and his beautiful daughter set out for the forest. They took with them many costly gifts for the parents of the bridegroom. But when the old king of the Shalwas heard what had brought them to his home, he was taken aback.

"But how can this be? he asked. "How will your heaven-sent daughter fare in this rough country? There are not maids to tend to her. And what shall we feed her? We eat the fruits of the forest. We sleep on an earthen floor."

Savitri took the blind old man by the hand, and spoke to him so sweetly and gently that she removed all his fears.

That same evening, when Satyavan returned from hunting, Savitri was given to him in marriage. The only guests were the hermits who lived nearby. All they brought as gifts were their blessings; and Savitri pleased them by removing

her jewels and replacing her rich garments with humble clothes.

The Lord-of-Horses bade his daughter farewell, and rode back alone to his kingdom.

The days and weeks and months slipped by, and it seemed to Satyavan that his wife grew lovelier and gentler by the hour. No man was as happy as he. Savitri, too, was happy; but as the day of doom approached, she became quiet and pensive. She decided she would not leave his side by day or night. So she watched and waited, and seldom slept.

One morning the blind old king asked Satyavan to go to a part of the forest where there was a bamboo grove. He asked him to cut and bring home several stout pieces of bamboo.

When Satyavan set out, Savitri decided to follow him.

Satyavan, whistling cheerfully, soon reached the place where the bamboos grew, and raised his axe; but he had scarcely lifted it above his head for the first stroke, when it fell from his hands. He sank to the ground.

Savitri, following close behind, knew that the fatal moment was at hand. She ran forward and took his head in her arms. A shadow fell over them, and she became aware of a terrible form bending over her. He was tall and gaunt, greenish in hue, but with eyes of a fiery red. He carried a noose in one of his hands.

This was Yama, the god of death.

Savitri rose slowly from the ground and bending low before Yama, said: "What do you want, oh mighty one?"

"I have come for Satyavan, whose term of life has ended." And Yama leant forward and drew the prince's soul right out of his body.

Then, turning to the south, he fled at lightning speed.

But Savitri, too, was fleet of foot. Love lent her wings, and she followed close at Yama's heels. They came at last to the edge of the world, beyond which no mortal may pass alive, and here the god of death stopped and spoke.

"Return, Savitri! You have followed far enough. Return and bury your husband's body with due rites."

"No, great Yama," answered Savitri. "When I wed my lord, I vowed to follow him, wherever he went or was taken. I have done no wrong since I made that vow, and so the gods have no power over me to make me break it."

"That is true," said Yama, "and your answer pleases me. Ask a boon of me — but not the gift of your husband's life!"

Savitri thought for a moment, and then asked that the old king of the Shalwas should regain his sight.

"It is granted," said Yama. "Now return. No mortal may pass this spot alive."

But Savitri stood her ground. She knew that no one loved Yama, that he was friendless even among the gods, so she decided to flatter him.

"Is it true, oh Yama, that a mortal is pleasing to the gods if she mingles with those who are virtuous?"

"It is true," said Yama.

"Then you cannot force me to go, for you are virtuous, and I become more pleasing to the gods every moment I stay beside you."

Yama was delighted, and told Savitri that, for her good sense, she might obtain another boon from him.

"Then grant that my father-in-law may regain his former kingdom," she said. Yama assented and told her for the third time to go back and find her husband's body before it was devoured by jackals.

"It does not matter," said Savitri, "if the jackals devour the corpse. Of what use is the body without the soul? Another body can be found for the soul, if it is released from your noose, but never another soul for the body."

"You speak with more wisdom than most mortals," said the god. "Yet one more boon will I grant you."

"Grant me a hundred sons, oh mighty Yama," cried Savitri. And when the god bowed his head in assent, she laughed and clapped her hands. "If you are indeed a god who keeps his word with men, then release the soul of Satyavan. There is no other man that I can marry, and only by bringing him back to life can you grant me the sons you have promised!"

Yama realised that Savitri had been allowed, by a greater power than he, to triumph over him; so he loosened the coil of rope, and Satyavan's soul flew up into the air and back to the forest were his body lay. Some time later, Savitri reached the same place and found her husband lying just as she had left him. As she lifted his head he opened his eyes and stretched himself and yawned.

"I must have fallen asleep," he said. "Why did you not wake me before? It is almost sunset."

Hand in hand they walked home, and on the way she told him all that had happened. And when they came home they found their father and mother rejoicing with the other hermits because the old man's sight had suddenly been restored. And even as they rejoiced a messenger arrived to say that the king's enemy had been slain and that the people wished their former ruler to return to them.

The next day Savitri and Satyavan, with their parents, returned to Shalwa, and there they all lived happily for the rest of their lives. We are told that Savitri and Satyavan lived together for four hundred years, and that they had a hundred sons, as Yama had promised.

Today, when anyone in India wishes to pay a wife the highest compliment, it is by saying that she is like Savitri, who brought back her husband's soul from the edge of the world.

RUSKIN BOND

The Tiger-King's Gift

LONG ago in the days of the ancient Pandya, kings of South India, a father and his two sons lived in a village near Madurai. The father was an astrologer, but he had never become famous, and so was very poor. The elder son was called Chellan; the younger Gangan. When the time came for the father to leave his earthly body, he gave his few fields to Chellan, and a palm leaf with some words scratched on it to Gangan.

These were the words that Gangan read:

From birth, poverty;
For ten years, captivity;
On the seashore, death;
For a little while happiness shall follow.

"This must be my fortune," said Gangan to himself, "and it doesn't seem to be much of a fortune. I must have done something terrible in a former birth. But I will go as a pilgrim to Papanasam and do penance. If I can expiate my sin, I may have better luck."

His only possession was a water-jar of hammered copper, which had belonged to his grandfather. He coiled a rope round the jar, in case he needed to draw water from a well. Then he put a little rice into a bundle, said farewell to his brother, and set out.

As he journeyed he had to pass through a great forest. Soon he had eaten all his food and drunk all the water in his jar. In the heat of the day he became very thirsty.

At last he came to an old, unused well. As he looked down into it he could see that a winding stairway had once gone round it down to the water's edge, and that there had been four landing places at different heights down this stairway; so that those who wanted to fetch water might descend the stairway to the level of the water and fill their water-pots with ease, regardless of whether the well was full, or three-quarters full, or half full or only one-quarter full.

Now the well was nearly empty. The stairway had fallen away. Gangan could not go down to fill his water-jar so he uncoiled his rope, tied his jar to it and slowly let it down. To his amazement, as it was going down past the first landing place, a huge striped paw shot out and caught it, and a growling voice called out: "Oh Lord of Charity, have mercy! The stair is fallen. I die unless you save me! Fear me not. Though king of tigers, I will not harm you."

Gangan was terrified at hearing a tiger speak; but his kindness overcame his fear, and with a great effort, he pulled the beast up.

The tiger king — for it was indeed the lord of all tigers — bowed his head before Gangan, and reverently paced round him thrice from right to left as worshippers do round a shrine.

"Three days ago," said the tiger king, "a goldsmith passed by, and I followed him. In terror he jumped down this well and fell on the fourth landing place below. He is there still. When I leaped after him I fell on the first landing place. On the third landing is a rat who jumped in when a great snake chased him. And on the second landing, above the rat, is the snake who followed him. They will all clamour for you to draw them up.

"Free the snake, by all means. He will be grateful and will not harm you. Free the rat, if you will. But do not free the goldsmith, for he cannot be trusted. Should you free him, you will surely repent of your kindness. He will do you an injury for his own profit. But remember that I will help you whenever you need me."

Then the tiger king bounded away into the forest.

Gangan had forgotten his thirst while he stood before the tiger king. Now he felt it more than before, and again let down his water-jar.

As it passed the second landing place on the ruined staircase, a huge snake darted out and twisted itself round the rope. "Oh, Incarnation of Mercy, save me!" it hissed. "Unless you help me,

I must die here, for I cannot climb the sides of the well. Help me, and I will always serve you!"

Gangan's heart was again touched, and he drew up the snake. It glided round him as if he were a holy being. "I am the serpent king," it said. "I was chasing a rat. It jumped into the well and fell on the third landing below. I followed, but fell on the second landing. Then the goldsmith leaped in and fell on the fourth landing place, while the tiger fell on the top landing. You saved the tiger king. You have saved me. You may save the rat, if you wish. But do not free the goldsmith. He is not to be trusted. He will harm you if you help him. But I will not forget you, and will come to your aid if you call upon me."

Then the king of snakes disappeared into the long grass of the forest.

Gangan let down his jar once more, eager to quench his thirst. But as the jar passed the third landing, the rat leaped into it.

"After the tiger king, what is a rat?" said Gangan to himself, and pulled the jar up.

Like the tiger and the snake, the rat did reverence, and offered his services if ever they were needed. And like the tiger and the snake, he warned Gangan against the goldsmith. Then the rat king — for he was none other — ran off into a hole among the roots of a banyan tree.

By this time Gangan's thirst was becoming unbearable. He almost flung the water-jar down the well. But again the rope was seized, and Gangan heard the goldsmith beg piteously to be hauled up.

"Unless I pull him out of the well, I shall never get any water," groaned Gangan. "And after all, why not help the unfortunate man?" So with a great struggle — for he was a very fat goldsmith — Gangan got him out of the well and on to the grass beside him.

The goldsmith had much to say. But before listening to him, Gangan let his jar down into the well a fifth time. And then he drank till he was satisfied.

"Friend and deliverer!" cried the goldsmith. "Don't believe what those beasts have said about me! I live in the holy city of Tenkasi, only a day's journey north of Papanasam. Come and visit me whenever you are there. I will show you that I am

not an ungrateful man." And he took leave of
Gangan and went his way.

From birth, poverty.

Gangan resumed his pilgrimage, begging his
way to Papanasam. There he stayed many weeks,
performing all the ceremonies which pilgrims
should perform, bathing at the waterfall, and
watching the Brahmin priests feeding the fishes
in the sacred stream. He visited other shrines,
going as far as Cape Comorin, the southernmost
tip of India, where he bathed in the sea. Then he
came back through the jungles of Travancore.

He had started on his pilgrimage with his copper water-jar and nothing more. After months of
wanderings, it was still the only thing he owned.
The first prophecy on the palm leaf had already
come true: "From birth, poverty."

During his wanderings Gangan had never once
thought of the tiger king and the others, but as
he walked wearily along in his rags, he saw a
ruined well by the roadside, and it reminded him
of his wonderful adventure. And just to see if the

Tiger King was genuine, he called out: "Oh king of tigers, let me see you!"

No sooner had he spoken than the tiger king leaped out of the bushes, carrying in his mouth a glittering golden helmet, embedded with precious stones.

It was the helmet of King Pandya, the monarch of the land.

The king had been waylaid and killed by robbers for the sake of the jewelled helmet; but they in turn had fallen prey to the tiger, who had walked away with the helmet.

Gangan of course knew nothing about all this, and when the tiger king laid the helmet at his feet, he stood stupefied at its splendour and his own good luck.

After the tiger king had left him, Gangan thought of the goldsmith. "He will take the jewels out of the helmet, and I will sell some of them. Others I will take home." So he wrapped the helmet in a rag and made his way to Tenkasi.

In the Tenkasi bazaar he soon found the goldsmith's shop. When they had talked awhile, Gangan uncovered the golden helmet. The goldsmith — who knew its worth far better than Gangan — gloated over it, and at once agreed to take out the jewels and sell a few so that Gangan might have some money to spend.

"Now let me examine this helmet at leisure," said the goldsmith. "You go to the shrines, worship, and come back. I will then tell you what your treasure is worth."

Gangan went off to worship at the famous shrines of Tenkasi. And as soon as he had gone, the goldsmith went off to the local magistrate.

"Did not the herald of King Pandya's son come here only yesterday and announce that he would give half his kingdom to anyone who discovered his father's murderer?" he asked. "Well, I have found the killer. He has brought the king's jewelled helmet to me this very day."

The magistrate called guards, and they all hurried to the goldsmith's shop and reached it just as Gangan returned from his tour of the temples.

"Here is the helmet!" exclaimed the goldsmith to the magistrate. "And here is the villain who murdered the king to get it!"

The guards seized poor Gangan and marched him off to Madurai, the capital of the Pandya kingdom, and brought him before the murdered king's son. When Gangan tried to explain about the Tiger King, the goldsmith called him a liar, and the new king had him thrown into the death-cell, a deep, well-like pit, dug into the ground in a courtyard of the palace. The only entrance to it was a hole in the pavement of the courtyard. Here Gangan was left to die of hunger and thirst.

At first Gangan lay helpless where he had fallen. Then, looking around him, he found himself on a heap of bones, the bones of those before him had died in the dungeon; and he was watched by an army of rats who were waiting to gnaw his dead body. He remembered how the tiger king had warned him against the goldsmith, and had promised help if ever it was needed.

"I need help now," groaned Gangan, and shouted for the tiger king, the snake king, and the rat king.

For some time nothing happened. Then all the rats in the dungeon suddenly left him and began burrowing in a corner between some of the stones in the wall. Presently Gangan saw that the hole was quite, and that many other rats were coming and going, working at the same tunnel. And then the rat king himself came through the little passage, and he was followed by the snake king, while a great roar from outside told Gangan that the tiger king was there.

"We cannot get you out of this place," said the snake king. "The walls are too strong. But the armies of the rat king will bring rice-cakes from the palace kitchens, and sweets from the shops in the bazaars, and rags soaked in water. They will not let you die. And from this day on the tigers and the snakes will slay tenfold, and the rats will destroy grain and cloth as never before. Before long the people will begin to complain. Then, when you hear anyone passing in front of your cell, shout: 'These disasters are the results of your ruler's injustice! But I can save your from them!" At first they will pay no attention. But after some time they will take you out, and at your word we will stop the sacking and the slaughter. And then they will honour you."

For ten years, captivity.

For ten years the tigers killed, the serpents struck, the rats destroyed. And at last the people wailed, "The gods are plaguing us."

All the while Gangan cried out to those who came near his cell, declaring that he could save them; they thought he was a madman. So ten years passed, and the second prophecy on the palm leaf was fulfilled.

At last the snake king made his way into the palace and bit the king's only daughter. She was dead in a few minutes.

The king called for all the snake-charmers and offered half his kingdom to any one of them who would restore his daughter to life. None of them was able to do so. Then the king's servants remembered the cries of Gangan and remarked that there was a madman in the dungeons who keeps insisting that the he could bring an end to all their troubles. The king at once ordered the dungeon to be opened. Ladders were let down. Men descended and found Gangan, looking more like a ghost than a man. His hair had grown

so long that none could see his face. The king did not remember him, but Gangan soon reminded the king of how he had condemned him without enquiry, on the word of the goldsmith.

The king grovelled in the dust before Gangan, begged forgiveness, and entreated him to restore the dead princess to life.

"Bring me the body of the princess," said Gangan.

Then he called on the tiger king and the snake king to come and give life to the princess. As soon as they entered the royal chamber, the princess was restored to life.

Glad as they were to see the princess alive, the king and his courtiers were filled with fear at the sight of the tiger king and the snake king. But the tiger and the snake hurt no one; and at a second prayer from Gangan, they brought life to all those they had slain.

And when Gangan made a third petition, the Tiger, the Snake and the Rat Kings ordered their subjects to stop pillaging the Pandya kingdom, so long as the king did no further injustice.

"Let us find that treacherous goldsmith and put him in the dungeon," said the tiger king.

But Gangan wanted no vengeance. That very day he set out for his village to see his brother, Chellan, once more. But when he left the Pandya king's capital, he took the wrong road. After much wandering, he found himself on the seashore.

Now it happened that his brother was also making a journey in those parts, and it was their fate that they should meet by the sea. When Gangan saw his brother, his gladness was so sudden and so great that he fell down dead.

And so the third prophecy was fulfilled.

On the sea-shore, death.

Chellan, as he came along the shore road, had seen a half-ruined shrine of Pillaiyar, the elephant-headed god of good luck. Chellan was a very devout servant of Pillaiyar, and, the day being a festival day, he felt it was his duty to worship the god. But it was also his duty to perform the funeral rites for his brother.

The seashore was lonely. There was no one to help him. It would take hours to collect fuel and driftwood enough for a funeral pyre. For a while Chellan did not know what to do. But at last he took up the body and carried it to Pyllaiyar's temple.

Then he addressed the god. "This is my brother's body," he said. "I am unclean because I have touched it. I must go and bathe in the sea. Then I will come and worship you, and afterwards I will burn my brother's body. Meanwhile, I leave it in your care."

Chellan left, and the god told his attendant *Ganas* (goblins) to watch over the body. These *Ganas* are inclined to be mischievous, and when the god wasn't looking, they gobbled up the body of Gangan.

When Chellan came back from bathing, he reverently worshipped Pillaiyar. He then looked for his brother's body. It was not to be found. Anxiously the demanded it of the god. Pillaiyar called on his goblins to produce it. Terrified, they confessed to what they had done.

Chellan reproached the god for the misdeeds of his attendants. And Pillaiyar felt so much pity or him, that by his divine power he restored dead Gangan's body to Chellan, and brought Gangan to life again.

The two brothers then returned to King Pandya's capital, where Gangan married the princess and became king when her father died.

And so the fourth prophecy was fulfilled:

For a little while happiness shall follow.

But there are wise men who say that the lines of the prophecy were wrongly read and understood, and that the whole should run:

From birth poverty;
For ten years, captivity;
On the seashore, death for a little while;
Happiness shall follow.

It is the last two lines that are different. And this must be the correct version, because when happiness came to Gangan it was not "for a little while." When the goddess of good fortune did arrive, she stayed in his palace for many, many years.